# Together

## Read more UNICORN and YETI books!

# Together

written by
**Heather Ayris Burnell**

art by
**Hazel Quintanilla**

SCHOLASTIC INC.

For Hil. We always have fun when we're together! — HAB

To my four-legged babies: Frida, Camila, Lucy, Catalina, Dante, Bruno, Luna, Jack, and Fiona, I love you. — HQ



Library of Congress Cataloging-in-Publication Data

Names: Burnell, Heather Ayris, author. | Quintanilla, Hazel, 1982-illustrator.
Title: Together / by Heather Ayris Burnell ; illustrated by Hazel Quintanilla.
Description: First edition. | New York, NY : Acorn, Scholastic Inc., 2022.|
Series: Unicorn and Yeti ; 6 | Summary: In three stories, friends Unicorn and Yeti spend time with each other, watching clouds in the sky, playing copycat, and having a tea party.
Identifiers: LCCN 2021001241 (print) | ISBN 9781338627756 (paperback) | ISBN 9781338627763 (library binding) |
Subjects: CYAC: Unicorns—Fiction. | Yeti—Fiction. | Friendship—Fiction. | Humorous stories.
Classification: LCC PZ7.B92855 To 2022 (print) | DDC [E]—dc23
LC record available at https://lccn.loc.gov/2021001241 LC

10 9 8 7 6 5 4 3 2 1 22 23 24 25 26

Printed in China 62

First edition, February 2022

Edited by Katie Carella
Book design by Sarah Dvojack

# Table of Contents

Zip! Zigzag! Zoom!. . . . 1

Copycorn. . . . . . . . . . . . . . . 22

Tea Party. . . . . . . . . . . . . . . 38

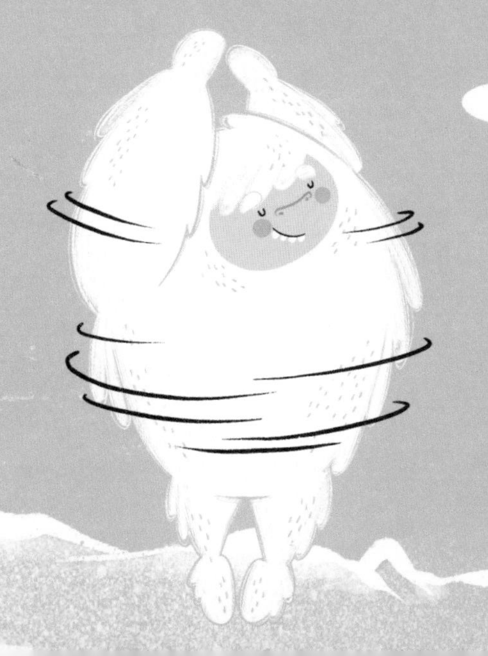

# Zip! Zigzag! Zoom!

Unicorn and Yeti looked up.

Wow!

The sky is big.

The sky is **very** big.

It makes me feel small.
It makes me feel **very** small.

Why do you think the sky is so big?
Hmmm.
Hmmm.

I do not know why it is so big, but I like it!
I like the warm sun in the sky.
Me too.

ZIP!
Oh no!
Brrr!

A cloud zipped
in front of the sun!

ZiP!
Now the cloud is not in front of the sun.
It zipped by!

How do clouds zip through the sky so fast?
The wind moves them.

Zigzag!

What are those dots zigzagging in the sky?

Those are seeds.

Seeds belong in the ground.
What are they doing up there?

They are flying!
But seeds don't fly.

The wind moves the seeds like it moves the clouds.
Where do you think the seeds are going?
To find a new place to grow.

I wonder where that will be.

They could go far
in the big sky!

Look at these bugs zooming around!

I would like to
zoom around.

Let's go!
Up with the bugs.
Up with the seeds.
Up with the clouds!

Zip!
Zigzag!
Zoom!

We do not zip like clouds.
We do not zigzag like seeds.
And we do not zoom like bugs.
No. But **we**
zip, zigzag, and zoom
like a unicorn and a yeti!

Whee!

# Copycorn

Unicorn saw Yeti bend to the side.

Unicorn saw Yeti leap.

Unicorn leaped.

Unicorn saw Yeti twirl.

Unicorn twirled.

What are you doing?
What are **you** doing?
I am dancing.
I am dancing **too**!

Dancing is fun.
Dancing is fun.

Ha ha ha!
Ha ha ha!
You are funny.
You are funny.

I am going to sit down.
I am going to sit down.

Let's play tic-tac-toe.
Let's play tic-tac-toe.

I will be O.
I will be O.

We can't both be O.

We can't both be O.

Why are you copying me?
Why are you copying me?
Stop it.
Stop it.

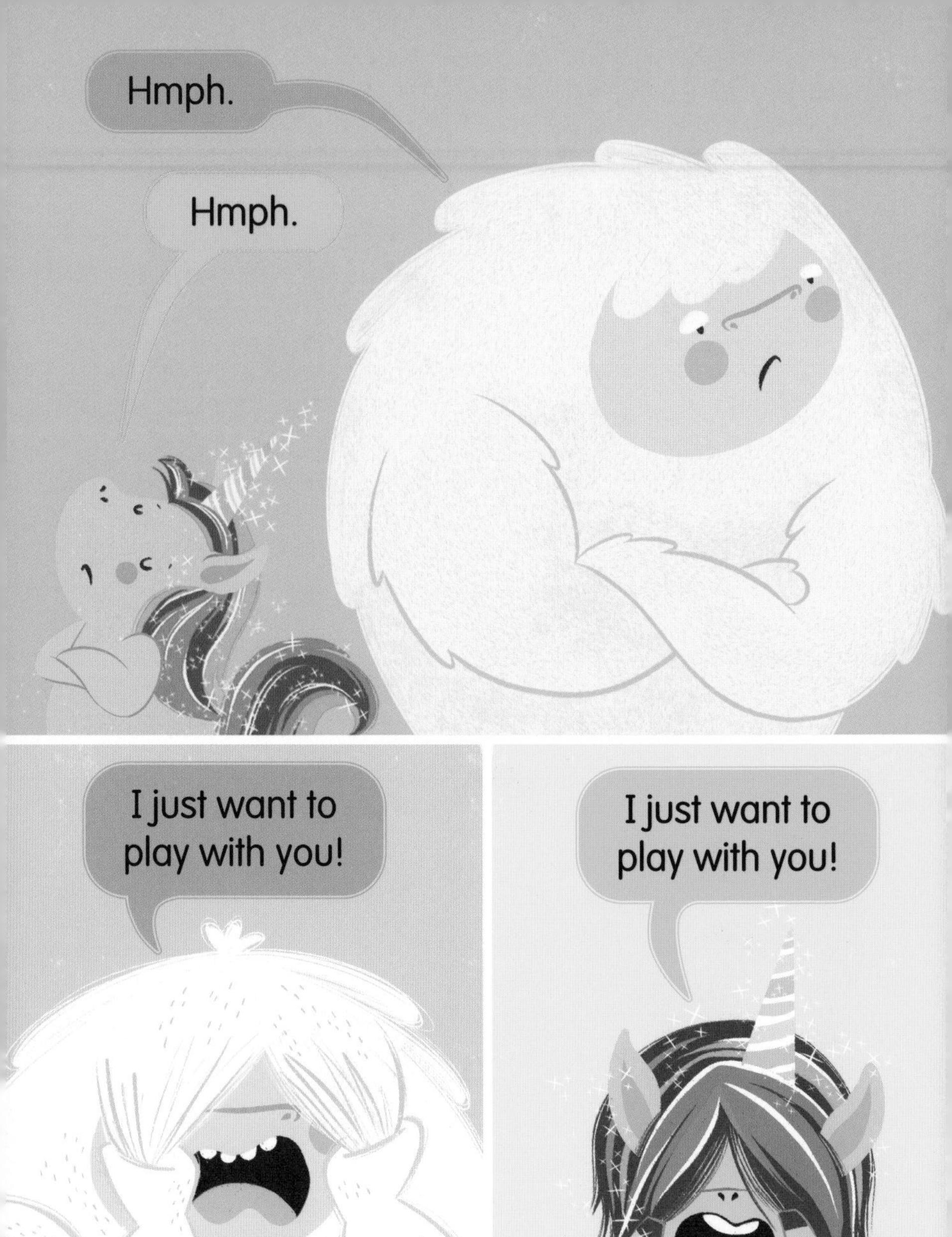
Hmph.
Hmph.
I just want to play with you!
I just want to play with you!

You are being a copycorn.
It is not fun.
I am sorry.
I **am** being a copycorn.
It is not fun for you.

Okay, it was
a little fun at first.
I was just being silly!

Are you copying **me** now?

Maybe **I** am
a copycorn!

Copy me!
Bend to the side.
Leap.
Twirl.

Copycorn!

# Tea Party

Let's have a tea party!

A tea party sounds fun!

Tea parties are fun. They are also fancy!
We can drink tea and be fancy together!

Let's drink tea!
Not yet!
The table is set, but **we** have to get ready.
How do we get ready for a tea party?

We need to dress up.
We should look fancy!
You can use magic
to make us fancy!

Too frilly.

Too formal.

Too fluffy.

Wow!

We look **very** fancy!

Now we can drink tea!
Wait!
When you have a tea party, you use good manners.
Oh.
Let me pull your chair out for you.
Thank you.

Oops.

Sorry!

It is okay.
Sigh.

May I pour you some tea?
Yes!

Yes . . . what?
Yes . . . please?
Thank you.

Would you like a cookie?
Yes please!

NOM
NOM
NOM

Eek!

You have frosting on your cheek.
You have crumbs all over.
We are a mess!

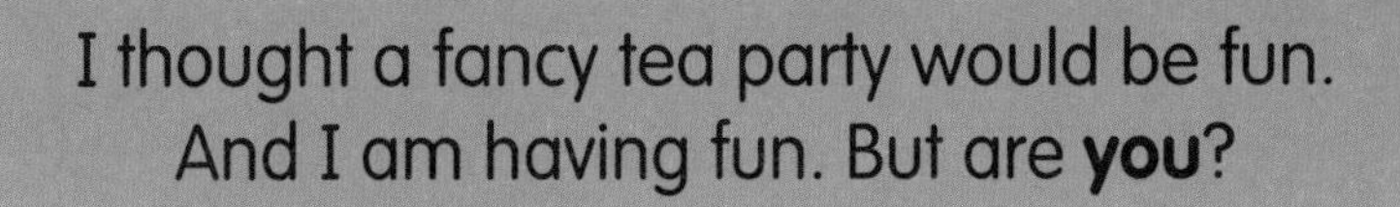


Well . . . no.

Our tea party would be more fun if you were having fun too.

I just wanted us to be fancy.

Maybe we need to wear
something else.

Let's change!

Ta-da!
Hats are fancy.
These fancy hats are just right for our tea party.

Can we drink tea now?
Of course!

Slurp!
Slurp!
Slurp!
Sip.
Sip.
Sip.

# About the Creators

**Heather Ayris Burnell** loves drinking tea, especially if it means she gets to dress up and have a tea party with a friend! Heather lives on a farm in Washington State where she likes to watch clouds, seeds, and bugs zip, zigzag, and zoom around in the sky. Heather is a librarian and the author of the Unicorn and Yeti early reader series.

**Hazel Quintanilla** lives in Guatemala. Hazel always knew she wanted to be an artist. When she was a kid, she carried a pencil and a notebook everywhere.

Hazel illustrates children's books, magazines, and games! And she has a secret: Unicorn and Yeti remind Hazel of her sister and brother. Her siblings are silly, funny, and quirky — just like Unicorn and Yeti!

# YOU CAN DRAW YETI IN A FANCY SUIT!

1. Draw one large oval for Yeti's body. Draw a circle for his face. (Draw lightly with a pencil! You will erase as you go.)

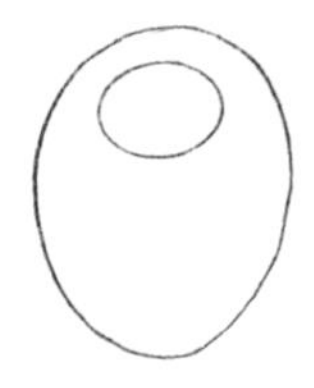

2. Add two ovals for Yeti's arms. One arm is bent, so draw a swoop to connect that arm to Yeti's body! Then add two soft triangles for his legs.

3. Draw fur on Yeti's forehead and on the top of his head. Give him eyebrows, a nose, and a smile!

4. Draw the outline of Yeti's jacket and pants. (Erase some body lines as you go.) Give him ovals for hands and add two furry feet!

5. Add details—such as buttons, stripes, fancy shoulder fringe, and rosy cheeks!

6. Color in your drawing!

## WHAT'S YOUR STORY?

Unicorn and Yeti dress up for a fancy tea party! Imagine **you** get to dress up and drink tea with them. What would you wear? How fancy would you be? Write and draw your story!

scholastic.com/acorn